Buster

the Very Shy Dog

By Lisze Bechtold

Green Light Readers
HOUGHTON MIFFLIN HARCOURT
Boston   New York

For Allen, William, Austin, and Beau

First Green Light Readers Edition, 2015

All rights reserved. Originally published as selections in *Buster the Very Shy Dog* by Houghton Mifflin Books for Children, an imprint of Houghton Mifflin Harcourt Publishing Company, 1999.

Green Light Readers and its logo are trademarks of Houghton Mifflin Harcourt Publishers LLC, registered in the United States of America and other countries.

For information about permission to reproduce selections from this book, write to Permissions, Houghton Mifflin Harcourt Publishing Company, 215 Park Avenue South, New York, New York 10003.

www.hmhco.com

The illustrations for this book were drawn in ink and painted in watercolors.

The Library of Congress has cataloged *Buster the Very Shy Dog* as follows:
Bechtold, Lisze.
Buster the very shy dog/Lisze Bechtold.
p. cm.
ISBN: 978-0-395-85008-4 hardcover
ISBN: 978-0-618-11122-0 paperback
Summary: In three stories, Buster the dog overcomes his shyness to make a friend, discovers his special talent, and helps Phoebe find the garbage bandits. [1. Dogs—Fiction. 2. Bashfulness—Fiction.]
I. Title.
PZ7.B380765Bu 1999 97-12452
[E] –dc21 CIP AC

ISBN: 978-0-544-33606-3 GLR paperback
ISBN: 978-0-544-33607-0 GLR paper over board

Manufactured in China
SCP 10 9 8 7 6 5 4 3 2 1
4500520609

CONTENTS

Buster's First Party

When Buster first came to Roger's house,
he was small and shy.

Phoebe, Roger's other dog, was not shy.
She was bossy.

The cats were bossy, too.

When Buster grew up, he was big and shy,
but he still felt small.

When someone came to visit,
Buster would run and hide.
Most people met Buster by accident.

One day a lot of people came to visit.
It was hard for Buster to find a place to hide.

"A party!" barked Phoebe.
"Roger's birthday party!"
"What is a party?" wondered Buster.
He watched as Phoebe made new friends
and helped herself to ice cream and cake.
"I wish I could have some ice cream and cake too,"
thought Buster, "but someone might see me."

When everyone went outside
to watch Phoebe do her fancy tricks,
Buster crept out from behind the couch.

He looked at the ice cream and cake.
He smelled the ice cream and cake.
He almost tasted the ice cream and cake.

But then someone shouted,
"Hey, look! Another dog! Can he do tricks, too?"

Buster ran and hid again,
until a little girl saw him.
"Here, doggy, doggy," she yelled.

Soon a long line of kids was following
Buster around and around the house.
"Here, doggy, doggy!" called the little girl.
"HERE, DOGGY, DOGGY!" called all the other kids.

Buster slipped under the back porch.
"I don't think I like parties," he sighed,
"except for the ice cream and cake."

After a while, Buster heard a sniffle,
then a little sob.
He peeked out.
When a little girl looked down at him,
Buster backed far away.

"Now she will say, 'Here, doggy, doggy,'" he thought.
But the girl did not say anything.
She just sat and cried.

Buster watched her
for a long time.

He wanted her to feel better,
but he did not know what to do.

Then Buster did something very brave.

After a while the girl talked to him.
"I don't know anyone at this party.
No one played with me.
Then that other dog ate all
of my ice cream and cake!"

Buster knew just how she felt.
"You are a nice dog," she said,
"much nicer than that other one.
Wait here." She ran into the house.
When she came back, the little girl said,
"Let's have ice cream and cake!"

Buster and Phoebe

Buster thought Phoebe was an amazing dog.
Phoebe was brave.

She was good at finding things.

Most of all,
she was an ace ball catcher.
She could catch any ball,
no matter how far

or how high
Roger threw it.
"Good dog, Phoebe!"
Roger always said.

Ever since Buster was a puppy
he had tried to be just like Phoebe.
But it was hard.
Buster was shy.

He was not good at finding things.

Most of all, he was not an ace ball catcher.
He could not catch any ball,
no matter how close
or how slowly
Roger threw it.

"It's okay," Roger told him.
"You are good at other things."
"I am?" thought Buster. "Like what?"
But Roger did not say.

"Every dog should be able to catch,"
Phoebe told Buster. "You just have to
keep your eye on the ball."
Buster tried keeping his eye on the ball.

It did not help.

"Phoebe is good at everything," he thought,
"and I'm not good at anything."

"I have an idea," said Phoebe. "Follow me."
She picked up her ball and ran to Roger's room.

"Maybe you need glasses," she said, "like Roger."

But glasses did not help.

The hamster cage crashed to the floor.
Roger woke up.
"Oh no!" he cried. "Where's Maxie?"

Roger looked all around the room for Maxie the hamster.

Phoebe sniffed all around the room for Maxie.

Buster slunk toward the door.
"I'm not good at finding things," he thought.

Phoebe gave up sniffing.

Roger flopped down on the bed.

"I've had Maxie ever since the fourth grade," he said.

"What if she is lost forever?"

Buster rested his chin on Roger's arm.

Roger sighed deeply. Buster sighed, too.

"Buster," said Roger, "you always listen to my troubles.

You are the best listener in this house."

"I am?" thought Buster. He wagged his tail.

Then he had an idea.

Buster listened all around the room.

He listened,

and listened,

and listened.

At last he heard a tiny munching sound
coming from the dresser.
He gently poked his nose into the open drawer.
There was Maxie the hamster.
"Good dog, Buster!" cried Roger.
"You are amazing!"